The Lost Crown of Meleor

written & illustrated by George Teply

When you look up in the sky on a clear night, you can see many shining dots. Some of them are stars, others are planets. One of those, this one, is the planet Meleor.

It is a beautiful planet, full of trees, lakes and rivers.

ANNICK PRESS • TORONTO • NEW YORK • VANCOUVER

Meleorites are the colorful creatures who live there. Today is Sunday on Meleor and you can see them going for a walk or talking with friends.

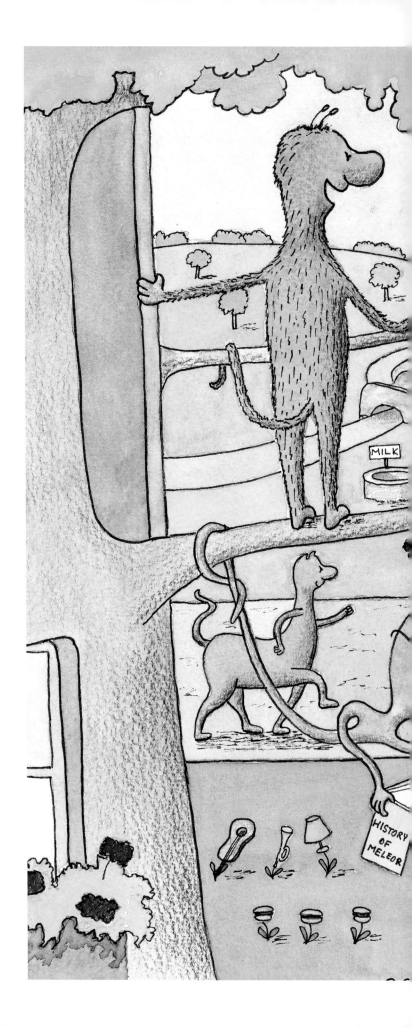

On other days Meleorites usually work in their
gardens. They grow house-trees to live in, food to
eat and toys to play with. They also grow things
like guitars and spaceships.

It is on this planet that the Crown of Meleor got
lost. Well, it didn't really get lost. Quikqueek
dropped it into a well.

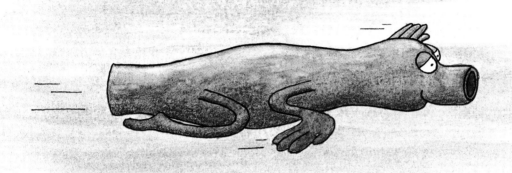

Which one is Quikqueek?

Quikqueek is the one who looks like a piece of purple rubber hose. A hose with big hands. And a big nose.

You can often see Quikqueek flying around Meleor like a jet plane.

Quikqueek's house-tree has a landing platform with a net for fast landings.

Smooth Koof and Bimbin the Hairy are Quikqueek's neighbors and friends.

Next to Koof and Bimbin lives their friend the Princess. On Sundays she wears the Crown of Meleor.

The Crown of Meleor is a beautiful royal hat. Meleorites grew it in a royal garden a long time ago.

To tell the truth, the Princess doesn't enjoy wearing the Crown. She is supposed to look dignified wearing it, and she hates looking dignified. Besides, the Crown is heavy.

But, according to a
tradition, the Princess
has to wear the Crown
every Sunday — and
that's what she does.

A tradition is a
tradition!

One Sunday morning the Princess went to pick
hot dogs for lunch. It was a hot day and the
Princess took off her Crown. She hung it on a
cheesecake tree.

Smooth Koof and Bimbin the Hairy were also out in their garden. The Princess stopped to talk with them. They talked about the nice weather they were having that day.

At that time Quikqueek was flying home from a toy orchard. He saw the Crown in the cheesecake tree. It would be fun, he thought, to try it on.

Quikqueek landed and put the Crown on his head. He looked at his reflection in a lemonade well.

And then it happened—just as Quikqueek came up with a very interesting silly face. The Crown slid off his head and disappeared in the lemonade!

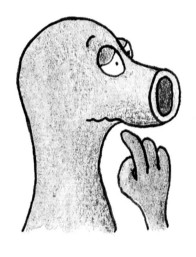

The Princess started saying that the sky was without a cloud. Instead, she said, "Here comes Quikqueek. What happened, Quikqueek? You don't look very happy."

"Princess," Quikqueek sniffled, "I have dropped your beautiful Crown into a well! What am I to do?"

The Princess didn't think it was such a big deal.

She said, "Don't worry, Quikqueek, it could happen to anybody. Besides, it shouldn't be difficult to fish the Crown out."

Several neighbors gathered around the lemonade well to see what was happening.

They had been out for a walk,

a slither,

a ride, a jog and a trot, but this was more interesting.

They all wanted to help, and that made Quikqueek feel good. That's what friends are for.

With so many friends helping, it really should be easy to fish the Crown out.

But it wasn't easy at all.

"We should get a magnet on a string," said someone.

"Why don't we empty the well and then climb down for the Crown," said another neighbor.

They tried it all, but nothing worked. And you should have seen the mess! Everybody was wet and sticky, with puddles of lemonade all over the place.

Quikqueek was heartbroken. And tired. Everyone was heartbroken and tired.

"I wish we could swim underwater," said Bimbin the Hairy. "Or under lemonade," he added.

"We learned in school that there are creatures who swim underwater," said Quikqueek. "They are called fish and they live on planet Earth."

"Hmm," said Smooth Koof. "Bimbin and I have grown a spaceship in our backyard. Someone could go to Earth and ask the fish for help."

"I have lost the Crown, so I should go," said Quikqueek.

"Good idea," said everybody.

"I will go with you, Quikqueek," said the Princess. "It'll be safer."

The neighbors brought fresh spaghetti, ice-cream and many other goodies from gardens and wells. The Princess and Quikqueek wouldn't be hungry on the way.

Quikqueek installed an antenna, and Bimbin and the Princess washed the windows. Koof made sure that everything was in order.

The spaceship was soon ready to go.

Quikqueek and the Princess flew to Earth. But instead of a fish, they brought back Jeff.

It was a nice day on Earth when Quikqueek and the Princess arrived.

Jeff, a fire-fighter, had been snorkelling that day.

Suddenly, like a giant pumpkin, a spaceship appeared in the sky.

"Hello there," Quikqueek called, "is this Earth?"

"Yes, it is," shouted back the surprised Jeff.

"And can you swim underwater?" Quikqueek asked.

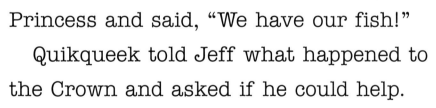

"Yes, I can," replied Jeff.

Quikqueek turned to the Princess and said, "We have our fish!"

Quikqueek told Jeff what happened to the Crown and asked if he could help.

Jeff said, "Sure, why not. Fire-fighters do these things all the time."

And there you have it: Jeff, and not a fish, travelled back to Meleor.

Quikqueek introduced himself and the Princess. He said, "It is our pleasure to welcome you aboard."

"Hi," said the Princess.

"Hi, I am Jeff and the pleasure is mine," replied Jeff.

Jeff liked it in the speeding spaceship. It was roomy and comfortable. There were windows all around.

Jeff saw beautiful stars and planets passing by, and a few comets too.

Jeff also learned how to pilot the spaceship. He only had to say "A little faster" or "More to the right," and the spaceship did exactly as told.

It was a pleasant trip.

Jeff didn't waste any time when they landed on Meleor. He put on his snorkel and dived into the lemonade.

Looking straight down through murky lemonade, he saw the sparkle of the Crown. This is going to be easy, he thought.

But it wasn't.

When Jeff reached for the Crown, it slipped away.

Jeff swam closer to see what was happening. No wonder — somebody was wearing it!

The creature smiled and said, "Hello."

"Blublu," said Jeff. Try to say "Hello" when you are upside down in lemonade.

"My name is Well Being," said the creature, "what's yours?"

Jeff wanted to say, "My name is Jeff," but to make it short he just said, "Blubf." He also wanted to say, "Give me the Crown, we have you surrounded!"

Before he could say it, though, Well Being said, "We better get up there and return the Crown to the Princess."

And so they did.

The Princess wore the Crown, but in all this excitement she forgot to look dignified. And nobody noticed. Or if they did, they didn't mind.

The Princess invited all the neighbors and friends for a treat. They had a cheesecake from the tree where it all started.

Well Being suggested, "If you like, Princess, I'll keep the Crown for you during the week. You'll have it back every Sunday morning, clean and polished to a high shine."

"What a great idea," said the Princess.

From that Sunday on, the Princess no longer had to remember where she left the Crown. If it's not on her head, it must be with Well Being. She likes it that way.

Well Being likes it that way too. He loves polishing the Crown. He also loves wearing it while swimming. What could be better!

What's more, the Princess no longer needs
to look dignified. And everybody likes that.

Quikqueek no longer plays with the Crown. But he still likes to make silly faces when nobody is looking.

Jeff stayed on Meleor for a few days and had a very good time.

Quikqueek, Koof, Bimbin and the Princess took him back to Earth last Thursday. If you saw the large pumpkin in the sky, it was Jeff coming home.

Meleorites asked Jeff to say hello to everybody on Earth and that you can come and visit them any time you want.

You can do that tonight in your dreams. And don't forget to tell them that you are not a fish.

©2000 George Teply (text and art)
Designed by Sheryl Shapiro.
The characters in *The Lost Crown of Meleor* are registered trademarks of George Teply.

Annick Press Ltd.

We acknowledge the financial support of the Canada Council for the Arts, the Ontario Arts Council, and the Government of Canada through the Book Publishing Industry Development Program (BPIDP) for our publishing activities.

Cataloguing in Publication Data

Teply, George
The lost crown of Meleor

ISBN 1-55037-601-2 (bound) ISBN 1-55037-600-4 (pbk.)

I. Title.

PS8589.E64L67 1999   jC813'.54   C99-930301-5
PZ7.R2655Lo 1999

The art in this book was rendered in mixed media.
The text was typeset in American Typewriter.

Distributed in Canada by:
Firefly Books Ltd.
3680 Victoria Park Avenue
Willowdale, ON
M2H 3K1

Published in the U.S.A. by Annick Press (U.S.) Ltd.
Distributed in the U.S.A. by:
Firefly Books (U.S.) Inc.
P.O. Box 1338
Ellicott Station
Buffalo, NY 14205

Printed in Hong Kong